June 2015

To Angelo:

Happy 2nd Birthday!

We love you!

From: Granny and Grandpa Dave

All Tucked In on SESAME STREET!

by Lillian Jaine
illustrated by Marybeth Nelson

SESAME STREET

sourcebooks jabberwocky

It's time for bed on Sesame Street,
but Elmo just can't get to sleep!

He's counted sheep from one to ten,
and then back down to one again.
But still he sits with open eyes
and looks out at the starry skies.

So now let's sing a special song
to help him sleep the whole night long!

Good night, sleep tight.

Don't let Twiddlebugs
steal the blanket tonight!

TWIDDLE
BUGS
WELCOME!

End the day with a bedtime treat,
something tasty, something sweet!

Take a bath with your favorite toy,
with bubbles that you'll both enjoy!

SOAP

SOAP

Now you're warm and dry—just right!
Brush your teeth all clean and white!

Pull on your jammies, the coziest pair.
At bedtime they're the thing to wear!

Read a book, and you will see
all the things that you can be.

Find a star and make a wish:
a bike, a book—perhaps a fish!

Now pull the covers up to your chin.
Look at that—you're all tucked in!

5 4 3 2 1
Start at five and count to one.
Turn out the lights when you are done!

Sleep comes in every shape and way.
It's the perfect end to a perfect day.

The time has come to close your eyes.
Each dream will bring a new surprise.

Sweet "sueños"!
That means "dreams"!

Good night, sleep tight.

Now our song is at an end.
The time has come for sleep, my friend.
Let's give our hugs, and kisses, too.
And then we'll say,

"Good night to you!"

Text by Lillian Jaine
Illustrations by Marybeth Nelson

Published by Sourcebooks Jabberwocky, an imprint of Sourcebooks, Inc.
P.O. Box 4410, Naperville, Illinois 60567-4410
(630) 961-3900
Fax: (630) 961-2168
www.jabberwockykids.com

Library of Congress Cataloging-in-Publication data is on file with the publisher.

Source of Production: Worzalla, Stevens Point. WI, USA
Date of Production: May 2014
Run Number: 5001666

Printed and bound in the United States of America.
WOZ 10 9 8 7 6 5 4 3 2 1